A PROMISE IS A PROMISE

Story·Robert Munsch & Michael Kusugak
Art·Vladyana Krykorka

Annick Press
Toronto • New York

Twentieth printing, July 2003

Annick Press Ltd.

We acknowledge the support of the Canada Council for the Arts,
the Ontario Arts Council, and the Government of Canada through
the Book Publishing Industry Development Program (BPIDP) for
our publishing activities.

Cataloging in Publication Data

    Munsch, Robert N., 1945-
      A promise is a promise

    ISBN 1-55037-009-X (bound)   ISBN 1-55037-008-1 (pbk.)

    I. Kusugak, Michael. II. Krykorka, Vladyana.
    III. Title.

    PS8576.U58P76 1988 jC813'.54 C88-093193-0
    PZ7.M86Pr 1988

Distributed in Canada by:
Firefly Books Ltd.
3680 Victoria Park Avenue
Willowdale, ON
M2H 3K1

Published in the U.S.A. by Annick Press (U.S.) Ltd.
Distributed in the U.S.A. by:
Firefly Books (U.S.) Inc.
P.O. Box 1338
Ellicott Station
Buffalo, NY 14205

Printed and bound in Canada by
Friesens, Altona, Manitoba.

visit us at: www.annickpress.com

On the very first nice day of spring Allashua said, "I'm going to go fishing. I'm going to go fishing in the ocean. I'm going to go fishing in the cracks in the ice."

"Ah, ah," said her mother, "don't go fishing on the sea ice. Under the sea ice live Qallupilluit. They grab children who aren't with their parents. Don't go fishing in the ocean. Go fish in a lake."

"Right," said Allashua, "I promise to go fishing in the lake and not in the ocean, and a promise is a promise."

So Allashua set out like she was going to go to the lake near her house, but when she got to the end of the street she didn't go to the lake. She walked down the long snowy path that led to the ocean.

At the edge of the ocean were large cracks where the tide broke and jumbled the ice. Allashua looked very carefully and did not see any Qallupilluit. She said, "On TV I have seen Santa Claus, Fairy Godmothers and the Tooth Fairy, but never any Qallupilluit. I think my mother is wrong."

But just in case her mother was right, Allashua stood beside the sea ice and yelled, "Qallupilluit have dirty noses." Nothing happened.

Allashua yelled, "Qallupilluit smell like a dead whale in the summer." Nothing happened.

Allashua walked right out onto the sea ice and yelled, as loud as she could, "Qallupilluit, Qallupilluit can't catch me!" Nothing happened. The only thing Allashua heard was the sound of snow blowing over the ice.

So Allashua got out her line and her hook. She walked over to a large crack in the ice and started to fish. Right away a fish grabbed the hook and Allashua pulled it up. She caught six fish in a row. Allashua yelled, "I am the best fisherman in the world!" And from behind her something said, with a voice that sounded like snow blowing over the ice, *"The best you may be, but the smartest you are not."*

Allashua turned around. There, between her and the shore, were the Qallupilluit. They looked at her and said, *"Have you seen the child who said Qallupilluit have dirty noses?"*

"Oh, no, Qallupilluit. I have seen no such child, and besides, your noses are very pretty."

"Have you seen the child who said we smell like a dead whale in the summertime?"

"Oh, no, Qallupilluit. I have seen no such child, and besides, you smell very nice, just like flowers in the summer."

"Have you seen the child who yelled, 'Qallupilluit, Qallupilluit can't catch me'?"

"Oh, no, Qallupilluit. I have seen no such child, and besides, my mother says that you can catch whatever you want to."

"Right," said the Qallupilluit. *"We catch whatever we want to, and what we want to catch right now is you."*

One grabbed Allashua by her feet and dragged her down, down, under the sea ice to where the Qallupilluit live.

The sea water stung Allashua's face like fire. Allashua held her breath and the Qallupilluit gathered around her and sang, with voices that sounded like snow blowing over the ice:

> *Human child, human child*
> *Ours to have, ours to hold.*
> *Forget your mother, forget your brother,*
> *Ours to hold under the ice.*

Allashua let out her breath and yelled, "My brothers and sisters, my brothers and sisters; I'll bring them all to the sea ice." For a moment nothing happened, and then the Qallupilluit threw Allashua up out of the sea into the cold wind of the ice and said, *"A promise is a promise. Bring your brothers and sisters to the sea ice and we will let you go."*

Allashua began to run up the long, snow-covered path that led to her home. As she ran her clothes started to freeze. She ran more and more slowly until she fell to the ground. And that is where Allashua's father found her, almost at the back door, frozen to the snow.

Allashua's father gave a great yell, picked up Allashua and carried her inside. He tore off Allashua's icy clothes and put her to bed. Then the father and mother got under the covers and hugged Allashua till she got warm. After an hour Allashua asked for some hot tea. She drank ten cups of hot tea with lots of sugar and said, "I went to the cracks in the sea ice."

"Ah, ah," said her family, "not so smart."

"I called the Qallupilluit nasty names."

"Ah, ah," said her family, "dumber still."

"I promised to take my brothers and sisters to the cracks in the sea ice. I promised to take them all to the Qallupilluit."

"Ah, ah," said her family, "a promise is a promise." Then her mother and father made some tea and they sat and drank it, and didn't say anything for a long time. From far down the snow-covered path that led to the sea the Qallupilluit began calling, *"A promise is a promise. A promise is a promise. A promise is a promise."*

The mother looked at her children and said, "I have an idea. Do exactly as I say. When I start dancing, all of you follow Allashua to the cracks in the sea ice." And the children all whispered to each other, "Ah, ah, why will our mother dance? This is not a happy time."

Allashua's mother went out the back door and yelled, "Qallupilluit, Qallupilluit, come and talk with me." And they did come, right up out of the cracks in the sea ice. Up the long, snow-covered path to the sea they came, and stood by the back door. It was a most strange thing, for never before had the Qallupilluit left the ocean.

The mother and father cried and yelled and asked for their children back, but the Qallupilluit said, *"A promise is a promise."*

The mother and father begged and pleaded and asked for their children back, but the Qallupilluit said, *"A promise is a promise."* Finally Allashua's mother said, "Qallupilluit, you have hearts of ice; but a promise is a promise. Come and join us while we say goodbye to our children."

Everyone went inside. First the mother gave her children some bread. She said to the Qallupilluit, "This is not for you." But the Qallupilluit said, *"We want some too."* The mother gave the Qallupilluit some bread, and they liked it a lot.

Then the mother gave each of her children a piece of candy. She said to the Qallupilluit, "This is not for you." But the Qallupilluit said, *"We want some too."* The mother gave the Qallupilluit some candy, and they liked it a lot.

Then the father started to dance. He said to the Qallupilluit, "This is not for you." The Qallupilluit said, *"We have never danced. We want to dance."* And they all started to dance. First they danced slowly and then they danced fast and then they started to jump and yell and scream and dance a wild dance. The Qallupilluit liked the dancing so much that they forgot about children. Finally the mother started to dance, and when the children saw their mother dancing they crawled out the back door and ran down the long, snowy path that led to the sea. They came to the cracks in the sea ice and Allashua whispered, "Qallupilluit, Qallupilluit, here we are."

Nothing happened. Then all the children said, "Qallupilluit, Qallupilluit, here we are."

Nothing happened.

Then all the children yelled, as loud as they could, "Qallupilluit, Qallupilluit, here we are!"

Nothing happened, and they all went back to the land and
sat on a large rock by the beach.

Two minutes later the Qallupilluit ran screaming down the
path and jumped into their cracks in the ice. Allashua stood up
on the rock and said, "A promise is what you were given and a
promise is what you got. I brought my brothers and sisters to
the sea ice. But you were not here. A promise is a promise."

The Qallupilluit yelled and screamed and pounded the ice till it broke. They begged and pleaded and asked to have the children, but Allashua said, "A promise is a promise." Then the Qallupilluit jumped down to the bottom of the sea and took their cracks with them, and the whole ocean of ice became perfectly smooth.

Then the mother and father came walking down the long, snowy path to the ocean. They hugged and kissed each one of their children, even Allashua. The father looked at the flat ocean and said, "We will go fishing here, for Qallupilluit have promised never to catch children with their parents, and a promise is a promise." Then they all did go fishing, quite happily. Except for Allashua. She had been too close to the Qallupilluit and could still hear them singing, with voices that sounded like blowing snow:

> *Human child, human child,*
> *Ours to have, ours to hold.*
> *Forget your mother, forget your brother,*
> *Ours to hold under the ice.*

The End

A Qallupilluq is an imaginary Inuit creature, somewhat like a troll, that lives in Hudson Bay. It wears a woman's parka made of loon feathers and reportedly grabs children when they come too near cracks in the ice.

The Inuit traditionally spend a lot of time on the sea ice, so the Qallupilluit were clearly invented as a means to help keep small children away from dangerous crevices.

Michael Kusugak, thinking back to his childhood in the Arctic, made up a story about his own encounter with the Qallupilluit. He sent it to Robert Munsch, who had stayed with Michael's family while telling stories in Rankin Inlet, N.W.T. *A Promise is a Promise* is the result of their collaboration.

For Adrian ~ J.D.

For Anna and Emily ~ L.M.

First published 2013 by Macmillan Children's Books
This edition published 2014 by Macmillan Children's Books
a division of Macmillan Publishers Limited
20 New Wharf Road, London N1 9RR
Basingstoke and Oxford
Associated companies throughout the world
www.panmacmillan.com

ISBN: 978-1-4472-4019-8

Text copyright © Julia Donaldson 2013
Illustrations copyright © Lydia Monks 2013
Moral rights asserted.

1 3 5 7 9 8 6 4 2

A CIP catalogue record for this book is available from the British Library.

Printed in China

Written by
Julia Donaldson

Illustrated by
Lydia Monks

SUGARLUMP
and the
Unicorn

MACMILLAN CHILDREN'S BOOKS

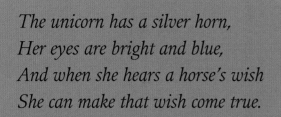

The unicorn has a silver horn,
Her eyes are bright and blue,
And when she hears a horse's wish
She can make that wish come true.

Sugarlump was a rocking horse.
He belonged to a girl and boy.
To and fro, to and fro,
They rode on their favourite toy.

"Here in the children's bedroom
Is where I want to be.
Happily rocking to and fro.
This is the life for me!"

But when the children were out at school
Sugarlump hung his head.
"Oh to be out in the big wide world!
I wish I could trot," he said.

"Done!" came a voice, and there stood a beast
With a twisty silver horn.
"I can grant horses' wishes,"
Said the snow-white unicorn.

She pawed the ground and tossed her mane
And flashed her eyes of blue.
Seven times she turned around,
And the horse's wish came true.

Now Sugarlump was a farmer's horse,
Pulling his cart and load.
Clippety-clop, clippety-clop,
He trotted along the road.

"Here in the open countryside
Is where I like to be.
Clippety-clop, clippety-clop,
This is the life for me!"

But time went by and the hills grew hard.
Sugarlump hung his head.
"Oh to be free of this heavy load.
I wish I could gallop!" he said.

"Done!" came the voice of the unicorn,
And she flashed her eyes of blue.
Seven times she turned around,
And the horse's wish came true.

Now Sugarlump was a racing horse
With a jockey on his back.
Gallop-a-jump, gallop-a-jump,
They thundered down the track.

"Here on this famous race course
Is where I like to be.
Gallop-a-jump, gallop-a-jump,
This is the life for me!"

But time went by and the jumps grew hard.
Sugarlump hung his head.
"Oh to slow down and have some fun!
I wish I could dance," he said.

"Done!" came the voice of the unicorn,
And she flashed her eyes of blue.
Seven times she turned around,
And the horse's wish came true.

Now Sugarlump was a circus horse
With his tail tied in a bow.
Dancing and prancing around the ring,
The star of every show.

"Here in this splendid circus
Is where I like to be.
Dancing and prancing, prancing and dancing,
This is the life for me!"

But time went by, and the children's cheers
Made Sugarlump hang his head.
"Oh for a child to ride me!
I want to go home," he said.

"Done!" came the voice of the unicorn,
And she flashed her eyes of blue.
Seven times she turned around,
And the horse's wish came true.

Sugarlump was a rocking horse,
But where were the girl and boy?
Time had flown and they both had grown
And forgotten their favourite toy.

Alone in the attic, Sugarlump sighed,
"I wish I had never been born!"

"But I have a better wish for you,"
Came the voice of the unicorn.

She pawed the ground and tossed her mane
And flashed her eyes of blue.
Seven times she turned around
And — the unicorn's wish came true!

Now Sugarlump is a fairground horse
On a beautiful merry-go-round.
Merrily up he rises
And merrily down to the ground.

"Here in this fabulous fairground
Is where I love to be.
Merrily, merrily, round and round,
This is the life for me!"

So Sugarlump is a happy horse.
The children are happy too . . .
And the unicorn with the silver horn
Closes her eyes of blue.